TOUCH, TASTE AND SMELL

Revised Edition
Steve Parker

Series Consultant
Dr Alan Maryon-Davis
MB, BChir, MSc, MRCP, FFCM

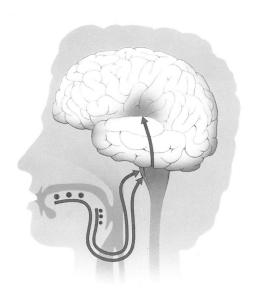

Franklin Watts
New York • Chicago • London • Toronto • Sydney

Words marked in bold appear in the glossary.

© **1989 Franklin Watts**
Original edition first published in 1982
First Paperback Edition 1991

Published in the United States by
Franklin Watts Inc.
95 Madison Avenue
New York, NY 10016

ISBN 0-531-10655-1 (lib.)/ISBN 0-531-24607-8 (pbk.)
Library of Congress Gatalog Card Number 88 51607

Illustrations: Andrew Aloof, Marion Appleton, The Diagram
Group, Howard Dyke, Hayward Art Group, David Holmes and
David Mallot.

Photographs: CONDOR is a registered trademark of British
Aerospace (Dynamics) Ltd 37; Colorsport 16; Chris
Fairclough 5, 22, 28, 29, 35; Royal National Institute for the
Blind 13; Science Photo Library; Cover – Hadjo CNRI; Eric
Graves 9; Martin Dohrn 11; Dr R Clark and M R Goff 15;
M I Walker 18, 31; Astrid Kage 24; Jan Hinsch 33; Eileen
Langsley, Supersport 21; ZEFA 19, 27.

Printed in Belgium

Contents

The role of the senses

We need to find out about our surroundings so we can carry out the essentials of life, such as finding food and avoiding danger. The parts of the human body that provide information about the outside world are called senses.

Humans use six main senses – touch, taste, smell, seeing, hearing and balance. Touch is a "multi-sense," which can detect heat, cold, pressure and pain as well as touch. Touch and certain other senses also tell the brain about conditions inside the body, such as its temperature, the amounts of body fluids and concentrations of certain chemicals.

Taste and smell were very important to early humans. They could not buy clean, healthy food from a supermarket. They did not even cook their food. Instead, they gathered nuts and berries from the countryside. Occasionally, they raided a bird's nest for eggs or hunted an animal for meat. The early humans relied on their senses of taste and smell to tell them if something was safe to eat or if it was poisonous or going bad.

Today, taste and smell are not quite so important to us. The food we grow or buy in stores is mostly safe to eat and cooking should kill bacteria and other germs and so make the food even safer. We use our senses of taste and smell more to appreciate a good meal than to detect if it will poison us. The organs that deal with taste and smell are the tongue and the nose. They are ideally positioned for their job to give "early warning" of trouble, just where food enters the body.

▷ When we eat and drink, we make use of several senses at the same time. We use taste and smell to appreciate the flavor of our food. Temperature and touch are also important, and affect our enjoyment of food. Enjoyment of strong-tasting or pungent-smelling foods has to be learned. Most children prefer mild tastes.

4

Nerve impulses

The job of each **sense** organ, such as the nose or the tongue, is to tell the brain about the information it has detected. To do this, each sense organ must change the information it receives into tiny electrical signals called nerve impulses.

Nerve impulses carry their information in a coded form, like the tiny bursts of electricity inside a computer. The impulses travel from the sense organs to the brain along nerves. In the brain, all the various impulses are sorted out, compared and interpreted – just as in a computer, but in a process many times more complicated.

The first stop for many impulses is the **thalamus**. This is a small region in the center of the brain. It helps to sort out the information from different sense organs and sends the impulses to various

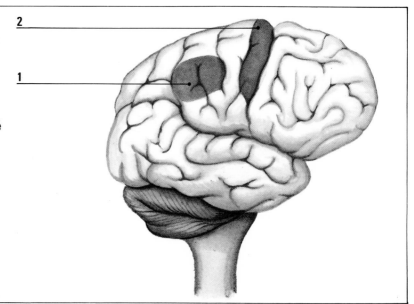

▷ Different sensations are handled by different areas on the surface of the brain.
1 Areas at the sides of the brain recognize sounds and tastes.
2 Sensations of touch received on the surface of the body are recognized in a band across the top of the brain.

parts of the brain. It is like a post office, which sorts out the letters it receives from different parts of the country and sends them to the correct addresses in a particular town.

Information from the sense organs is sent to various parts of the **cortex**. This is the large, folded area, which covers the top and sides of the brain. It is only a few millimeters thick, and flattened out it is about the area of a pillow case.

Impulses from each sense are always sent to one area of the cortex. This is called the center for that sense. The taste center is a small area on the side of the brain and the smell center, also quite small, is just below it. Touch is a more important and complicated sense, so it has a larger area, which runs in a band over the top of the brain.

▽ The relative importance of the different senses can be seen by measuring the area they take up on the surface of the cortex. The large area for touch taken up by face, nose, eyes and fingers can be clearly seen.

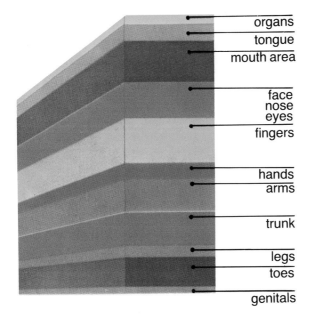

organs
tongue
mouth area
face
nose
eyes
fingers
hands
arms
trunk
legs
toes
genitals

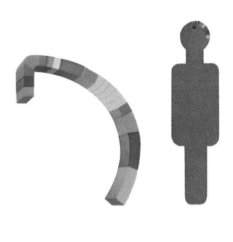

Receptors in the skin

Unique fingerprints

The ridges on the skin of the fingertips give a better grip than smooth skin. The pattern of ridges is different in every person. Fingerprints left at the scene of the crime by a careless criminal have been used to prove that the criminal was there – no other person could have made the prints. In some cases "poreprints" have also been used. These are prints left by the tiny openings of the sweat pores in fingertip skin. There are around 10–20 pores on each millimeter of ridge skin. Normally the sweat from the pores moistens the skin, to improve the grip. Try picking up a pin after thoroughly washing and drying your fingers!

The skin is the largest sensory organ of the body. In an average adult, it weighs about 4 kg (nearly 9 lb) and is some 2 sq m (about 20 sq ft) in area. It covers the body like a flexible, protective, showerproof, all-around overcoat.

The skin detects not only touch, but also pressure, pain and temperature. It has many other jobs too, such as keeping body fluids in, keeping dangerous substances out, protecting delicate internal parts of the body and helping to regulate body temperature.

The uppermost layer of the skin is very thin, only 1 mm (1/25th in) or so thick. It is mostly dead and cannot feel anything at all. The **receptors**, the various microscopic organs that detect touch, pressure and so on, are buried beneath this dead, protective layer. They are in the next layer down, which is very much alive.

A receptor is activated by a **stimulus**. With the skin, the stimulus might be a light touch or a hot saucepan handle. Without a stimulus, the receptors send impulses at a slow rate to the brain. When they receive a stimulus, the receptors send a fast succession of nerve impulses, like a burst of machine-gun fire, to the brain. In general, the stronger the stimulus, the faster the receptors produce their impulses. The brain detects which area of the body has been stimulated, which receptors are firing and how fast they are firing. When this information is put together, we "feel" what has happened.

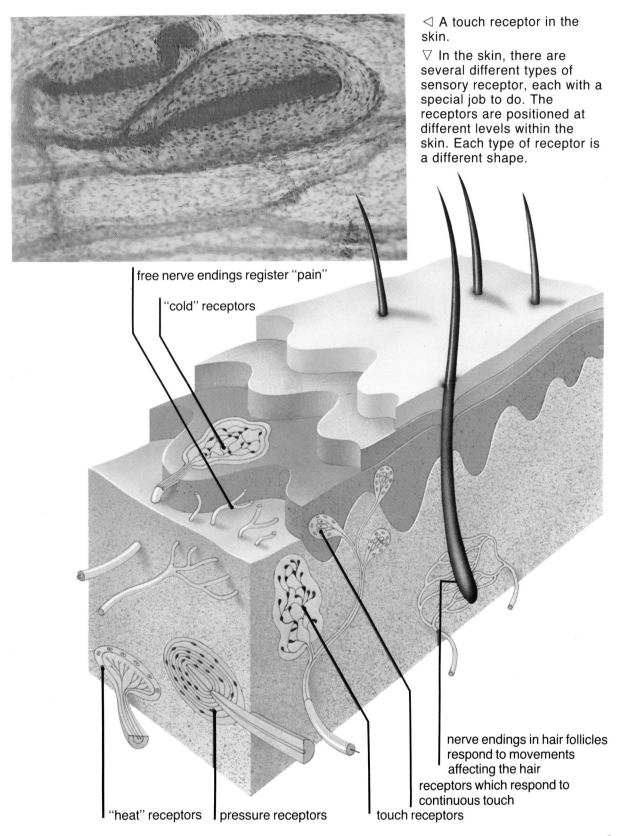

◁ A touch receptor in the skin.

▽ In the skin, there are several different types of sensory receptor, each with a special job to do. The receptors are positioned at different levels within the skin. Each type of receptor is a different shape.

free nerve endings register "pain"

"cold" receptors

nerve endings in hair follicles respond to movements affecting the hair

receptors which respond to continuous touch

"heat" receptors

pressure receptors

touch receptors

How touch works

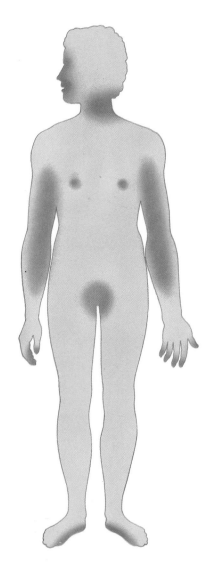

△ Touch receptors are clustered together in groups on the body. The areas shaded in green have the largest number of receptors and are the most sensitive parts of the body.

Some areas of the skin, especially the lips and fingertips, are much more sensitive than other areas, such as the back or the thigh. We use these "super-sensitive" areas to find out detailed information about the shape, texture, hardness and temperature of things we touch.

These areas are so sensitive because they have many receptors clustered together in the skin. Even the smallest stimulus is likely to trigger at least a few receptors. You can feel this for yourself. Find a pair of dividers, or compasses, and set the points about 25 mm (1 in) apart. Close your eyes and ask a friend to touch one of your fingertips gently with both points. You will probably feel the two separate points. Ask the friend to reduce the distance between the two points by a few millimeters and try again. (It is best to press on a slightly different patch of skin each time.)

Keep doing this until you can only feel one point. On the fingertips, this usually happens when the distance between the two points is about 2 mm ($\frac{1}{12}$th in). Your friend could occasionally press with one point, to make sure you are not cheating! Now repeat the experiment on your upper arm or lower leg. You may have to increase the distance between the two points to more than 50 mm (2 in) before you feel the points separately. These areas of the body have far fewer touch receptors so it is less likely that both divider points will stimulate them. By doing this type of experiment all over the body, a "sensitivity map" of the skin can be drawn.

Under the microscope, most touch receptors look like tiny onions. They have several layers of a jelly-like material. When they are squeezed, the layers rub against each other, which generates electrical nerve impulses.

The hairs that grow out of the skin are made of hard, dead, insensitive tissue. But wrapped around the living root of each hair, buried in the skin, is a web of nerves. This is a type of touch receptor. Moving the hair stimulates the nerves to fire off a burst of nerve impulses. When something brushes against us, it may not actually touch the skin, but if it bends the hairs, we will sense it. When you feel "the wind on your face," it is really the wind rocking the very fine hairs there. And when a hair is pulled out by the root, the nerve endings register pain.

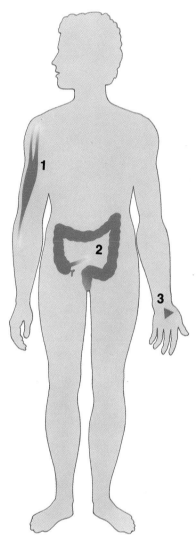

Goose pimples

In many animals, body hairs take part in temperature control. When temperature receptors in the skin and inside the body detect a drop in temperature, the hairs stand up straight. This traps air between the hair and the skin and helps to insulate against the cold. The movement of the hairs causes the familiar **goose pimples** or goose flesh, especially on the arms and legs, in people.

△ Receptors of various types are scattered throughout the body. They convert physical changes, such as pressure on the skin or the stretching of a muscle, into nerve signals.
1 Stretch receptors in muscles monitor the position of the limbs and body.
2 Receptors in the digestive system monitor the passage of food.
3 Receptors in joints monitor how much the joint is bent.

11

Aspects of touch

Touch helps to protect the body. If we grip something hard, and it feels as though it is cutting into the skin, we quickly let go. We also let go of something if we feel the pressure is likely to damage a muscle or a **tendon**. Our muscles are strong enough to tear themselves or damage the tendons that connect them to the bones they move.

Several diseases affect the touch receptors or the nerves that carry impulses from the receptors to the brain. This can cause trouble, because the person with the disease might not know when the skin is at risk. One such disease is **leprosy**. Leprosy sufferers are in danger of damaging their skin by touching things that are too hot or too sharp because they do not feel the warning signs of heat and pain. In some rare nerve diseases the sense of touch is lost in certain parts of the body.

▽ If the fingers are crossed, and a pea or other small object is gripped between them, it feels as if we are touching two separate objects. The brain cannot understand that a single object can touch the opposite sides of two fingers. This simple experiment shows how the "mental map" we have of our bodies can trick us in an unusual situation.

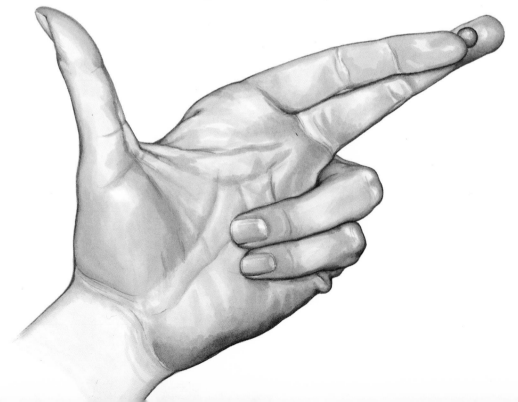

A person who has had a limb amputated may sometimes "feel" the limb, even though it is not there. This "**phantom limb**" may be itchy, painful, hot or cold. Although the receptors for these sensations have gone, parts of the nerves that carried their impulses to the brain are still in the stump. The scar tissue that grows over the cut ends of the nerves may stimulate them to send nerve impulses to the brain. The brain still "remembers" where these impulses came from originally and the person imagines the limb is still there.

The fingernails may also help with our sensitivity to touch. The nail acts as a hard, rigid "backboard" for the very sensitive skin of the fingertips. Without it, when we touch something, the flesh of the fingertip would bend back and fewer receptors might be stimulated. This would reduce our sensitivity to touch.

Seeing with the fingertips

It is wrong to think that blind people improve their other senses to compensate for their lack of sight. However, they do become better at interpreting the information they receive from their senses. One of the most important senses for the blind is the sense of touch. Sometimes, blind people can form a picture of what someone looks like just by touching that person's face.

◁ The **Braille** alphabet is made up of patterns of raised dots. By touching these patterns, blind people can read with their fingertips. The Braille alphabet was invented by a blind Frenchman, Louis Braille, in 1837.

Temperature control

Humans are "warm-blooded" animals. This means the human body tries to keep its temperature the same, no matter how hot or cold the surroundings are. The average body temperature is 36–37.2°C (97–99°F), which is warmer than all but the hottest places on Earth. This is why we say we are "warm-blooded."

Temperature receptors within the body, like those in the skin, help to control its internal temperature. If the temperature falls, then we feel cold. We put on more clothes, or move to a warmer place. If this does not work, the blood vessels in our skin become narrower so that less "warm" blood is carried near the surface of the body. This reduces the heat loss, but makes us look pale. Also, some of our muscles may twitch on their own. We call this "**shivering**" and it helps to generate heat (see Factbox on p. 11 about goose pimples).

If our body temperature rises, then we may take off some clothes or move to a cooler place. To help us cool down, the blood vessels in the skin widen and carry more blood. This gets rid of extra heat and we look red and flushed. The sweat glands in the skin release watery **sweat**, which evaporates from the surface and draws heat from the body.

The skin is also involved in detecting external temperature. Touching something very hot can burn, and intense cold can destroy our tissues. The receptors seem to be more sensitive to *changes* in temperature rather than to the actual temperature itself.

Temperature control

Occasionally, the body's mechanism for keeping itself warm or cool fails. Unless we are careful to guard against extreme temperature conditions the resulting problems can become very serious.

- **Hypothermia** A problem that often affects old people in cold conditions. Hypothermia occurs when the body temperature falls below 35°C (95°F). Many bodily processes stop working below this temperature and hypothermia can kill.
- **Hyperthermia** This is the condition in which the body temperature rises above 41°C (106°F). Symptoms include coma or convulsions and hot, dry skin. Hyperthermia may also kill.

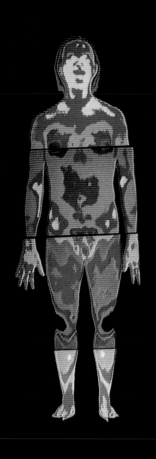
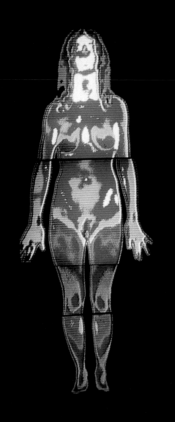
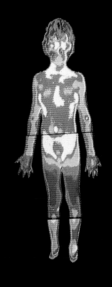
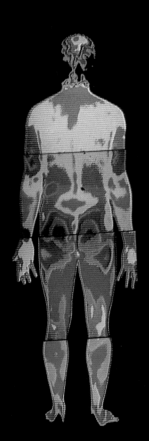
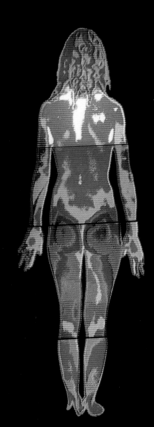

This **thermograph** was taken using special heat-sensitive film. The colors show the different temperatures of each part of the body. White shows the hottest areas, and then the colors change through red, orange, green and blue to purple, which represents the coolest parts. The temperature distribution differs in man, woman and child.

Pain – our warning system

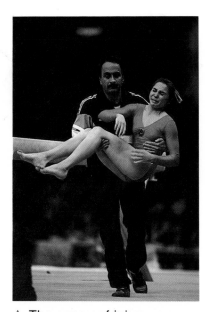

△ The agony of injury: a gymnast is carried from the hall after injury at the 1988 Seoul Olympics. Pain is a warning sign. It is often wise to abandon a performance at once, rather than try to struggle on and make any damage worse. However, at the time, the feeling of being out of the competition after so much practice can cause greater upset than the pain itself.

There is an old saying, "A little pain never hurt anyone." Like many old sayings, it sounds odd, but it is partly true. We may dread feeling pain, but this sense is vitally important. It helps to protect the body. If we feel pain, it warns us that the body is in danger of being damaged or may already be suffering damage, and we should take action right away.

We feel pain when various types of receptor are stimulated too much. There are also special pain receptors scattered about on the surface of the skin and body. They are densely clustered in very delicate areas, such as the surface of the eye. On the fingertips, there are fewer pain receptors. This is partly because the fingertips have so many touch and pressure receptors, and their main function is to detect light touch.

There are also pain receptors inside the body. These warn us if we strain a muscle, sprain a joint, break a bone, or if we are suffering from an illness. Sometimes the pain they register is vague and we are unable to pinpoint its position.

We have a variety of names for different sorts of pain. We describe pain as burning, aching, sharp, dull or shooting. It is impossible for us to feel someone else's pain and so discuss and agree on which kind of pain is which. Yet most people seem to be able to describe their own pain accurately. Doctors use a patient's description of what a pain feels like to help them diagnose an illness and prescribe the correct treatment.

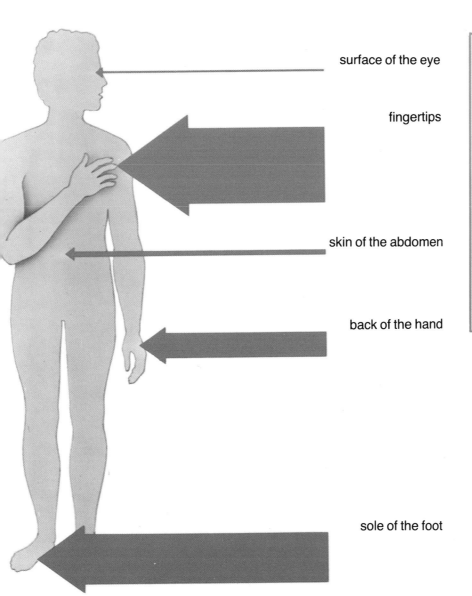

surface of the eye

fingertips

skin of the abdomen

back of the hand

sole of the foot

Sensitivity to pain

Pain receptors are distributed unevenly across the body, so different parts of the body require different amounts of pressure before they register pain. For example, it takes very little pressure to register pain in the eye. The fingertip would require 1,500 times more pressure to do so. Again, the amount of pressure causing pain to the back of the hand is a third of the pressure required on the fingertip.

The amount of pressure on the skin needed to cause pain varies enormously in different parts of the body. In this diagram the amount of pressure which causes pain is shown by the size of the colored arrows.

Blocking pain

Local anesthesia

Anesthesia is used to stop us feeling pain, usually during operations. Local anesthetics are used when we want to prevent pain from being registered in only one part of the body, for instance, when you are having a tooth filled. A drug is normally injected into the affected area or applied to the surface of the skin. This temporarily prevents the pain receptors in that area from functioning. Unlike a general anesthetic, a local anesthetic does not cause the patient to lose consciousness.

If someone has a pain and takes a pain-killing drug, an **analgesic**, or has an **anesthetic** (see box), the pain is relieved. Yet the cause of the pain may still be there. The actual sensation of pain "exists" only in the mind – that is to say, in the brain. This is why pain, more than most other senses, is linked with what goes on in the brain.

We can learn to ignore a certain amount of pain. And, if we are concentrating on something else, we may not notice pain. Soldiers have been wounded while saving a fallen comrade in battle, but they have not felt the pain of the wound until later. In a similar way, we can learn to expect pain, for example when we visit a dentist. If we are waiting to be hurt, the pain can feel much worse.

▷ This microscope picture shows nerve cells in the spinal cord. The cord collects nerve impulses which register pain from all over the body and passes them on to the brain. The brain can instruct groups of nerve cells, called **ganglia,** to stop some of these "pain" impulses from reaching it.

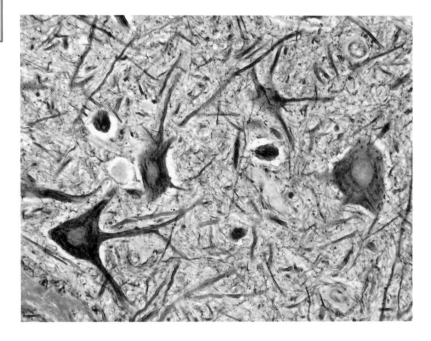

This happens because the brain can "switch off" or "dampen" pain under certain circumstances. Part of the mechanism for doing this is linked to the **spinal cord**, which can block some of the "pain" nerve impulses before they pass up to the brain.

Body chemicals called **endorphins** have been discovered in the brain and spinal cord. These are part of the mechanism which affects our perception of pain. They also alter the types of emotions linked with pain, such as worry and fear. Their name comes from endogenous, meaning "within the body," and **morphine**, a strong, pain-killing drug whose chemical structure resembles the endorphins. The first endorphins were isolated and identified by scientists in 1975.

△ Enormous effort is needed in top-class competition, as shown by these hurdlers. Sometimes the sheer physical effort and the stamina needed can merge into the feeling of pain. Athletes, such as long-distance runners, can learn to overcome this "pain-barrier" and improve their performance even further – provided they are not injured.

Muscles and reflexes

Close your eyes, and clap your hands. How did you know, without looking, that your hands would come together? In the body's muscles and tendons there are receptors called **proprioceptors**. These detect the amount of stretch in a muscle, showing whether it is contracted and short, or relaxed and long. In turn, this shows the position of your body and limbs.

The brain receives impulses from proprioceptors all over the body. Putting together the information, it constructs a "mental picture" of the posture and position of each part of the body. This

▽ Joints contain special receptors, which provide information about the position of the limb.

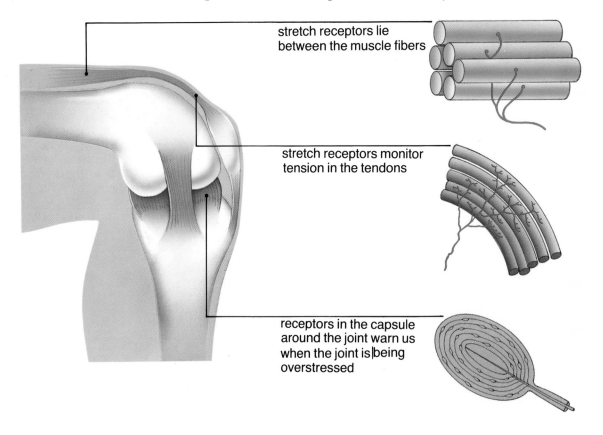

stretch receptors lie between the muscle fibers

stretch receptors monitor tension in the tendons

receptors in the capsule around the joint warn us when the joint is being overstressed

20

proprioceptive sense is sometimes called the kinesthetic sense. For much of the time, proprioceptors work along with your sense of balance. They keep track of your muscles and movements, making them smooth and balanced.

However, your brain is usually too busy to be involved in this continuous process. So proprioception is largely automatic. It works by a system of **reflexes**. As you move part of the body, the proprioceptors detect this and send nerve impulses to the spinal cord. More impulses are sent out right away, telling other muscles to move certain parts and keep you balanced. Sometimes, the system can be fooled. In the knee-jerk reflex, the proprioceptors send out impulses meaning (falsely) that you are falling backward. The reflex makes your knee straighten automatically.

▽ Proprioceptors in the muscles, tendons and joints make us aware of the positions of our body and limbs. Feats of balance, like this gymnast's hand-stand, involve split-second feedback from the body's senses, including proprioceptors, balance and eyesight, to the muscles which control and steady movements.

Linked senses – taste and smell

We smell with our noses, and taste with our tongues. The nose detects odor molecules floating in the air, while the tongue detects flavor molecules dissolved in a watery solution.

These two senses are very closely linked. When we eat food, the "taste" is really a combination of taste and smell. The reason is that food in the mouth gives off some odor molecules into the air. These travel up the connecting passage between the mouth and the nose, and into the large space inside the nose (the **nasal cavity**). The smell receptors in the nasal cavity are stimulated by the odor molecules.

▷ Smell can trigger various reactions in the body. When we are hungry, the smell of cooking stimulates the brain, which instructs salivary juices to flow into the mouth, in anticipation of chewing food. This is why we say a meal smells "mouth-watering."

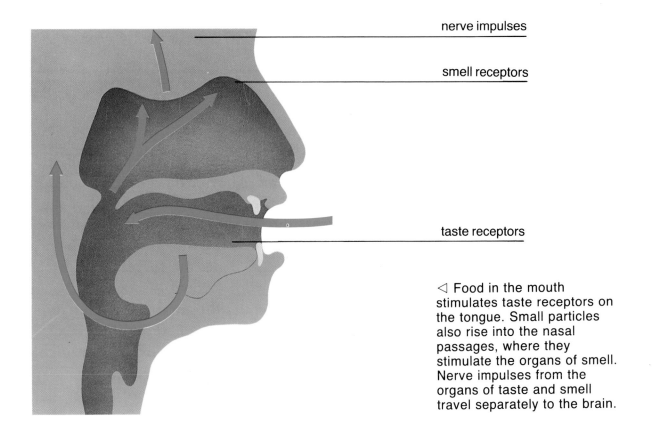

nerve impulses

smell receptors

taste receptors

◁ Food in the mouth stimulates taste receptors on the tongue. Small particles also rise into the nasal passages, where they stimulate the organs of smell. Nerve impulses from the organs of taste and smell travel separately to the brain.

When you have a cold, you may have noticed that food loses its flavor. This is because your nose is blocked by sticky **mucus**. Air cannot circulate, the smell receptors are smothered and your sense of smell cannot contribute to your sense of taste.

In a similar way, we can often "taste" a smell. This is because odor molecules float from the nose down into the mouth. Here, some of the molecules dissolve in the watery saliva coating the tongue and stimulate the taste receptors on the tongue. Animals such as snakes use this process to "taste the air" with their flicking tongues.

Originally, taste and smell had a very basic job – to tell the brain whether food was suitable to eat. These senses are dealt with by parts of the brain involved in other basic body urges, such as hunger and thirst.

Inside the nose

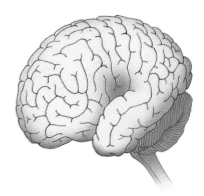

△ Information from the sense of smell is interpreted in a small area on the surface of the brain.

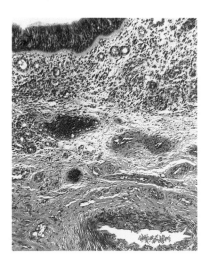

△ This microscope picture shows a section of skin from the nasal cavity. The purple area at the top of the picture is the tissue where the olfactory cells are located. Below this is a layer of tissue containing **nerve fibers** and blood vessels.

The parts of the nose that detect odors are called the **olfactory organs**. They cover an area about the size of a thumbnail, which is in the roof of the nasal cavity, roughly behind the bridge of the nose.

Every time you breathe in, air flows through the nasal cavity. Shelves of bone, the **turbinates**, direct the air rearward so it flows down through the back of the mouth and into the throat. Some of the air floats past the olfactory organs and any odor molecules are caught by the sticky mucus coating these organs. The molecules pass through the mucus and are detected by tiny sensory hairs, which stick out from the olfactory organs.

Like other sense organs, the hairs turn the stimulus (odor molecules) into electrical nerve impulses. The impulses pass up through the skull bone covering the roof of the nasal cavity, to nerve relay stations called the olfactory bulbs. From here, they travel straight to the smell center on the side of the brain.

As you breathe, you continually monitor odors in the air. This warns you of any unusual smells, which could be dangerous. A really bad smell may cause you to hold your nose or even vomit, since it might be from food you had already eaten, which was in fact bad.

If you want to smell something in more detail, you take a good sniff. This brings more air high into the nasal cavity, into contact with the olfactory organs. More odor molecules are detected, and so the smell is stronger.

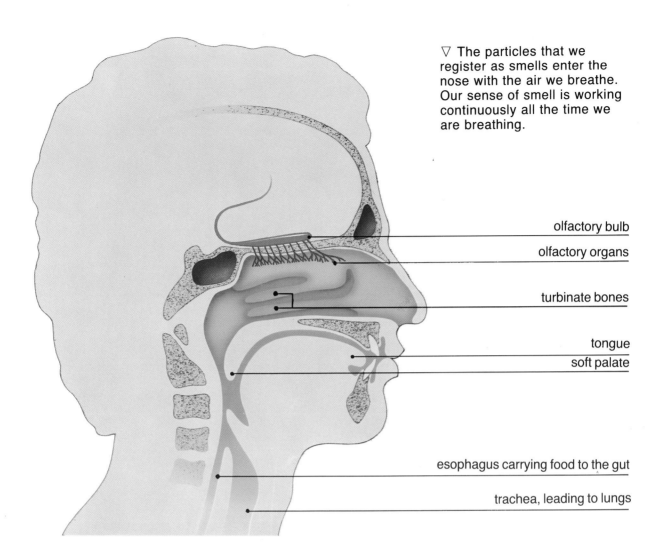

▽ The particles that we register as smells enter the nose with the air we breathe. Our sense of smell is working continuously all the time we are breathing.

olfactory bulb

olfactory organs

turbinate bones

tongue

soft palate

esophagus carrying food to the gut

trachea, leading to lungs

△ In normal breathing, air passes directly into the back of the throat.

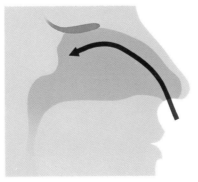

△ When we sniff, air eddies upward and flows over receptors in the top of the nasal cavity.

The sense of smell

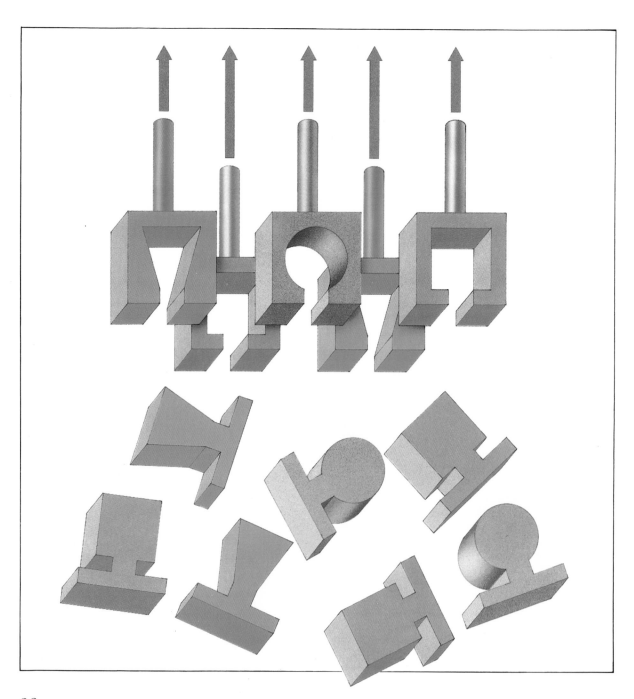

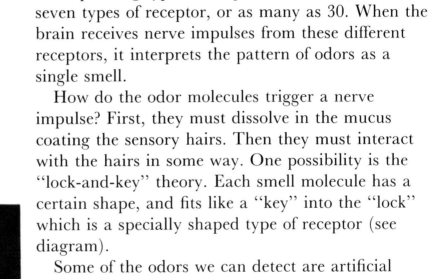

◁ It is thought that "smelly" substances are made up of molecules that have characteristic shapes. These latch on to particular receptors, causing them to produce nerve impulses. This is called the "lock-and-key" theory.

△ The smell of a wine is known as its "bouquet." Some wine-tasters are able to tell where and when a wine was made simply by sniffing it.

Scientists do not know exactly how our sense of smell works. There may be several basic types of odor molecules and each particular "smell" may be made up of a mixture of different types of odor molecule. Each type may be detected by a corresponding type of receptor. There may be only seven types of receptor, or as many as 30. When the brain receives nerve impulses from these different receptors, it interprets the pattern of odors as a single smell.

How do the odor molecules trigger a nerve impulse? First, they must dissolve in the mucus coating the sensory hairs. Then they must interact with the hairs in some way. One possibility is the "lock-and-key" theory. Each smell molecule has a certain shape, and fits like a "key" into the "lock" which is a specially shaped type of receptor (see diagram).

Some of the odors we can detect are artificial ones that do not occur in nature. The reason we are able to "smell" these artificial odors may be that their molecules just happen to resemble the odor molecules produced by natural substances.

In humans, smell is some 10,000 times more sensitive than taste. On average, we can detect and distinguish about 3,000 different smells. Experts, like wine-tasters or perfume-makers, who use their sense of smell in their work, do not have especially sensitive noses. They are able to concentrate on, identify and remember the odors they receive. They have a trained brain rather than a "trained nose."

The sensitive nose

△ Most people find the natural scents of flowers, the countryside and the seaside very pleasing. Many smells are stored in the memory. If we detect the same odors again many years later, this can bring back a strong "memory picture" of the first time we encountered the smell.

Sometimes, our sense of smell gets desensitized. If we walk into a house where several pets live, we might notice their smells at once. Yet, after a while, the smells seem to fade. The olfactory organs, like the other sense organs, respond mainly to changes in stimuli. The people who live in the house may become so used to the smells that they do not notice them unless they happen to go away for a while.

Once we become used to a smell, it may have to increase in strength up to 300 times before we are aware of it again. This is a sensible arrangement. Our surroundings give off so many smells that the brain would be swamped trying to keep track of them all. It is a good example of how our sense organs are selective and how the brain acts as a filter. Only information about a change in the smells of our surroundings, which may be important, gets through to the brain and is noticed.

Compared to other animals, humans do not have an especially good sense of smell. We have about five million smell receptor cells, each with some six sensory hairs. A dog may have the same area of olfactory tissue, but packed into it are 100 million receptor cells, each with 100 or more sensory hairs. This is why dogs can track people and sniff out certain substances, such as drugs.

Compared to many other animals, humans today have limited uses for their noses. We sniff food and drink, to appreciate their flavors. We also register the kinds of smells that warn us to keep away,

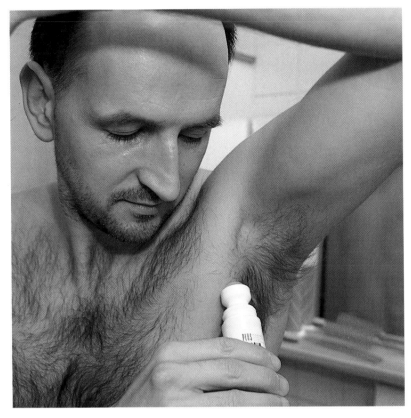

◁ Some odors are a natural part of the human body, but in today's world we may try to cover them up or replace them with other scents. This is partly due to what we are taught – that body odors are "unnatural" and to be avoided. However, strong body odors may mean that a person has poor hygiene, with the possibility of carrying dirt and disease.

perhaps because of a fear of disease – such as the odors of untreated sewage! Many other animals use smells much more widely. They may mark their territories with strongly-smelling urine or droppings, or with a scent secretion from special glands. Some animals attract mates using scents.

Some insects have an amazing sense of smell. A male moth can detect the odors given off by a female moth over a mile away. She gives off this scent trail to attract a mate. Smells like this, which stimulate an animal to do something, are called **pheromones**. The word is similar to hormones, which are the body's internal chemical messengers. Pheromones are external chemical messengers, and they exert their action at a distance. Humans have pheromones in their sweat and other body secretions – although we are not always aware of the effect they have on us!

The organs of taste

Taste is literally "on the tip of the tongue" as well as on the sides and back of the tongue. These are the four areas that are most sensitive to taste. Each part detects one or more of the four main flavors of food – sweet, salt, sour and bitter.

If we eat something that tastes bad, we may pull a face (a signal to others that this food is to be avoided) or even spit it out. This is how the sense of taste helps to protect the body against taking in poisonous or contaminated food. We vividly remember a bad taste, as we do a bad smell.

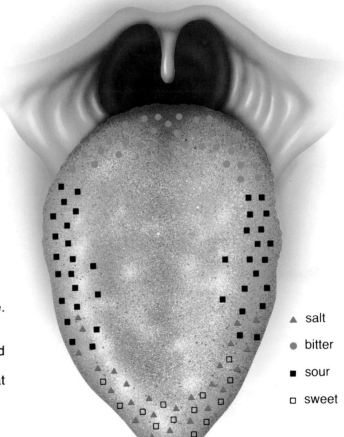

▷ The organs of taste are located mostly on the tongue. They are grouped according to the tastes they perceive. Sweet and salt are registered at the front of the tongue, sour at the sides and bitter at the back.

▲ salt

● bitter

■ sour

□ sweet

30

The receptors that detect taste are called **taste buds**. Each taste bud is a group of up to 30 tall, slender cells that fit together like the segments of an orange. The flavor molecules find their way into the center of the orange through a hole in the top.

The cells that make up taste buds only do their job for a few days. Like other cells on the "surface" of the body, they are continually being worn away and replaced by new ones made by the process of cell division.

An adult may have up to 10,000 taste buds. Most are on the tongue. Here they are grouped together into tiny **papillae**, which you may just be able to see with a magnifying lens. There are as many as 200 taste buds on one papilla. Other taste buds are found at the very back of the mouth and down into the throat.

A baby has more taste buds than an adult. As we grow old, the number of taste buds decreases. Elderly people tend not to detect the flavor of food as well, and some of them may lose interest in eating as a result.

▽ Taste receptors are grouped together into structures called papillae, which can be seen on the surface of the tongue as small bumps or specks. In the microscope picture (below left) are several taste buds. They are embedded into the surface of the tongue and are oval in shape.

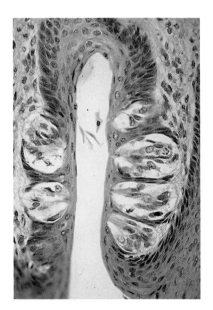

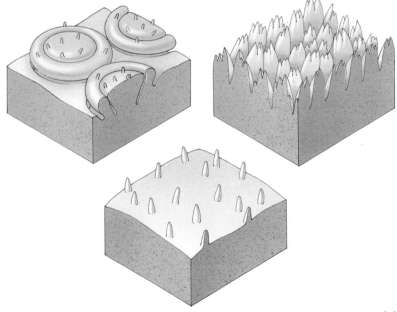

How taste works

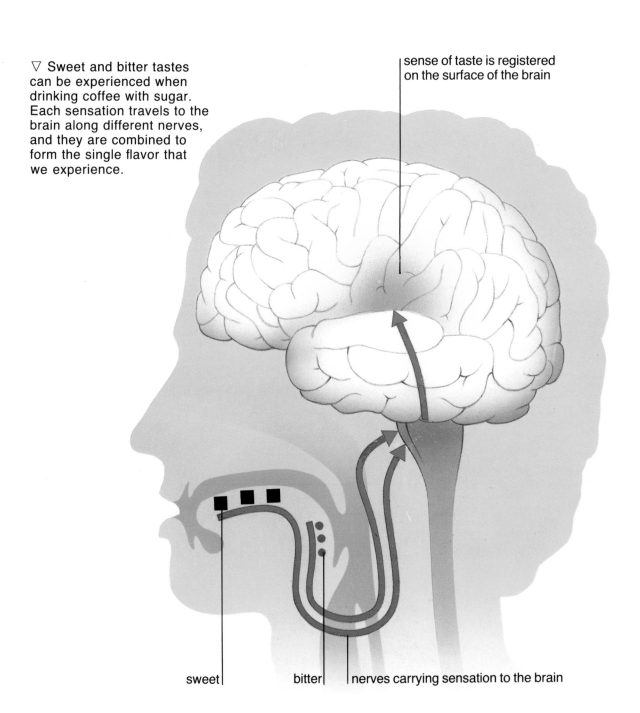

▽ Sweet and bitter tastes can be experienced when drinking coffee with sugar. Each sensation travels to the brain along different nerves, and they are combined to form the single flavor that we experience.

sense of taste is registered on the surface of the brain

sweet

bitter

nerves carrying sensation to the brain

We soon become used to strong tastes, as we do to powerful smells. When we eat a highly-spiced meal, the first mouthfuls seem very strong or "hot." However, as the taste buds become filled with flavor molecules, and the brain becomes used to the spicy sensation, we tend not to notice it so much.

It is thought that the receptor cells of the taste buds may respond to the shape of the dissolved flavor molecules in that same "lock-and-key" fashion in which the nose receptors may detect odors. This could also explain why new chemical substances, not formed in nature, seem to taste of naturally-occurring foods – their molecules have similar shapes.

But this does not explain all the aspects of taste. Most acid substances have a sour taste, although their molecules have very different shapes. We detect as "salty," substances that break up into electrically-charged particles when they dissolve. It may be that taste also has something to do with the chemical and electrical nature of the flavor molecules themselves.

Taste sensations are sent to the brain relatively slowly. We usually perceive smell before taste. The position of the taste buds also makes a difference. Sweet and salty flavors, detected mainly on the tip of the tongue, are usually first to register in the brain. Bitter flavors may not be fully felt until the food passes over the main bitter-sensing taste buds, at the back of the tongue. This may leave a bitter after-taste in the mouth.

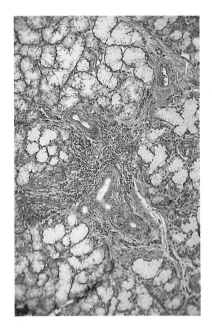

△ This microscope photograph shows clumps of cells from a salivary gland, in the mouth. There are six salivary glands, and they make the watery fluid called saliva that coats the inside of the mouth. Flavor molecules dissolve in the saliva on the tongue, so that the taste buds can identify the molecules. Saliva is also mixed with food as we chew, to lubricate the food and make it easy to swallow.

33

Fooling the senses

Food additives

Although we usually know whether or not the thing we are about to eat is wholesome, some manufactured foods contain ingredients that could be harmful to us. We are unable to detect these additives with our senses of taste or smell. Here are three food additives:

- Tartrazine is a chemical used to color foods yellow. It is added to some canned vegetables, custards, smoked fish and various drinks. It may make certain people more susceptible to asthma or skin rashes.
- Erythrosine is used to color foods red. It is used in some cake mixtures and tinned fruits. It may interfere with the body's hormones, and possibly make some children over-active and "on edge."
- Chlorine has been used to bleach some foods and to preserve them. It can be found in some types of bread and flour. Chlorine is a powerful chemical and is banned as a food additive in many countries.

In our daily life, we are usually able to use all our senses. When we sit down to a meal, our eyes see the food. The nose smells it. The skin and the inside of the mouth detect its temperature, hardness and texture. The tongue tastes its flavors. The impression we get is a combination of all these senses.

The impression is also affected by previous experience. The brain remembers sights, sounds, smells, tastes and feelings, and links them all together. Foods that are a different color from normal may not be tasted correctly. A yellow drink that contains strawberry flavoring confuses the senses, because the color and taste do not match.

You can show how closely the senses of touch, taste and smell are linked, by carrying out an experiment to remove each sensory clue in turn. Ask a friend to help you. Take some common foods, such as an apple and a potato, and cut them up into pieces. Ask your friend to tie a blindfold around your eyes and try eating the pieces of food with your fingers. (The proprioceptors in your muscles will enable your fingers to find your mouth without seeing!) The two foods will probably be quite easy to identify, because you can feel their textures with your fingers as well as being able to smell and taste them.

Next try eating the pieces of food with a fork. You cannot feel the food with your fingertips, so it should be slightly more difficult to identify it correctly. Now try eating the food while holding your nose. The identification test will be even more difficult this time. Finally, mash each piece into a pulp so that its natural texture is destroyed. Now you have only taste as a clue. And, by this time, you will be getting used to the flavors of apple and potato. You may well find the two foods impossible to tell apart. However, a new, strong taste, with a different texture, such as a spoonful of lemon juice, will have a remarkable effect!

Touch, taste and smell, like our other senses, are designed to tell us important things about the world around us. The brain can ignore most of their information, most of the time. However, a sudden change, such as feeling a hot flame or smelling something burning, can alert us to a possible source of danger – and maybe save our lives.

▽ Many manufactured and processed foods contain **additives** such as artificial flavorings or colorings. These make the food look good to eat or make it taste like foods we recognize. A few people may be especially sensitive to certain of these chemicals, and after eating the food may develop a headache or skin rash.

35

Super-sensitive machines

Modern technology has provided us with many machines that can out-perform our own senses of touch and smell. For instance, engineers use machines called accelerometers to measure vibrations too small for our fingertips to detect. The electronic type of accelerometer passes an electric current through special crystals. If the crystals are compressed or stretched by minute vibrations, they cause a change in the electric current. Accelerometers are used in space rockets and satellites, to measure any vibrations which might upset the delicate electronic circuits.

"Sniffing" machines that are much more sensitive than the human nose have also been developed. These machines are used to detect substances such as drugs in aircraft luggage. Traditionally, dogs have been used for this purpose and to a great extent are still used today.

One type of drug-detecting machine draws in air through a tube, rather like a large vacuum cleaner, and passes the air through a chemical sensor. The sensor is "tuned in" to detect specific substances.

Another type of sniffing machine is based on a synthetic resin which absorbs odor molecules from the air. The resin is left at a test site for a certain length of time. Then later, back in the laboratory, it is treated to make it release the odor molecules into another machine called a gas chromatograph. This can detect concentrations of certain substances down to fractions of parts per million.

◁ "Sniffing machines" at ports and airports "smell" cargoes and detect fumes given off by drugs, explosives, alcohol and other suspicious substances – no matter how tightly they are packed. CONDOR (Contraband Detector System) sucks samples of air from around suitcases or parcels (below) and feeds them along a tube into a truck. This contains a device called a mass spectrometer which analyzes the odors in the air. CONDOR's computers pick out the "smell fingerprints" of illegal substances from the many normal smells in air, and give a result in two minutes. A smaller, more mobile "hoover" device (left) draws air samples into its canister. The samples are taken to the main truck for analysis. If suspicious smells are detected, the cargo is then searched by hand.

Glossary

Additive: substance not found naturally in a food, but added during processing to help preserve it or change its flavor or color.

Analgesic: drug that reduces or blocks feelings of pain (a pain killer).

Anesthetic: drug that blocks all sensations, including touch and pain, so that the anesthetized part goes "numb."

Braille: special form of raised "writing" developed to allow the blind to read. Consists of patterns of raised dots making up letters and words.

Cortex: the pale gray surface layer of the brain, in which information is processed. Much of the brain's activity takes place in the cortex.

Endorphin: body chemical that acts as a "natural pain killer" and helps to lessen or block pain sensations.

Ganglia: small groups of nerve cells, in which some information can be processed and acted upon, without involving the brain. Some reflexes are controlled in ganglia near the spine.

Goose pimples: hairs on human arms or legs stand up straight when receptors in the skin detect a drop in temperature. This traps air between the hair and the skin and helps to insulate against the cold.

Hyperthermia: type of "heatstroke," when the body temperature rises above about 41°C (106°F).

Hypothermia: dangerous condition in which the body temperature falls to below about 35°C (95°F).

Leprosy: disease usually occurring in the tropics, in which bacteria damage the nervous system. Can result in serious damage to the hands and legs, due to its effect on the senses of touch, pain and temperature.

Morphine: powerful analgesic (pain killing) drug made from opium.

Mucus: sticky, watery material secreted from special glands. It protects and lubricates delicate surfaces, including the inside of the nose.

Nasal cavity: space in the skull, behind the nose, through which inhaled air passes on its way to the lungs.

Nerve fiber: special cell capable of passing an electrical signal, or nerve impulse, along its thread-like length.

Olfactory organs: the organs of smell, positioned in the top of the nasal cavity.

Papillae: small bumps on the surface of the tongue on which the taste buds are positioned.

Phantom limb: "feeling" that an amputated limb is still there, because the nerves that supplied the limb are still intact from the stump to the brain.

Pheromones: chemical messengers which cause a response in the organs of smell. Pheromones are produced in our perspiration, but we are not normally conscious of their presence.

Proprioceptor: microscopic organ which detects the stretching in a muscle or tendon. It allows the brain to be aware of the exact position of our limbs.

Receptor: structure that responds to a stimulus like touch or smell, and causes a nerve impulse to be generated.

Reflex: automatic response of the body to a stimulus. This allows a rapid response without involving the brain. Many reflexes serve to protect us from a possibly dangerous stimulus.

Sense: a body organ or collection of organs that informs us of some aspect of the outside world, such as sounds (hearing) or odors (smell).

Shivering: automatic "twitching" of muscles when we are cold, that generates heat and helps to warm the body.

Spinal cord: thick bundle of nerve fibers running up the spine, and joining on to the brain.

Stimulus: an event which can cause a response in the nervous system, such as pain, touch, heat, etc.

Sweat: perspiration, a salty fluid produced in tiny glands in the skin that helps to cool the body.

Taste buds: groups of taste receptor cells in the mouth, mostly on the tongue.

Tendon: tough ropy material that connects muscle to bone.

Thalamus: small area in the brain through which most of the information received from the sense organs passes.

Thermograph: special color-coded photograph taken with heat-sensitive film in which the different colors represent different temperatures.

Turbinates: thin shelves of bone in the nasal cavity which guide the air and direct its flow.

Index